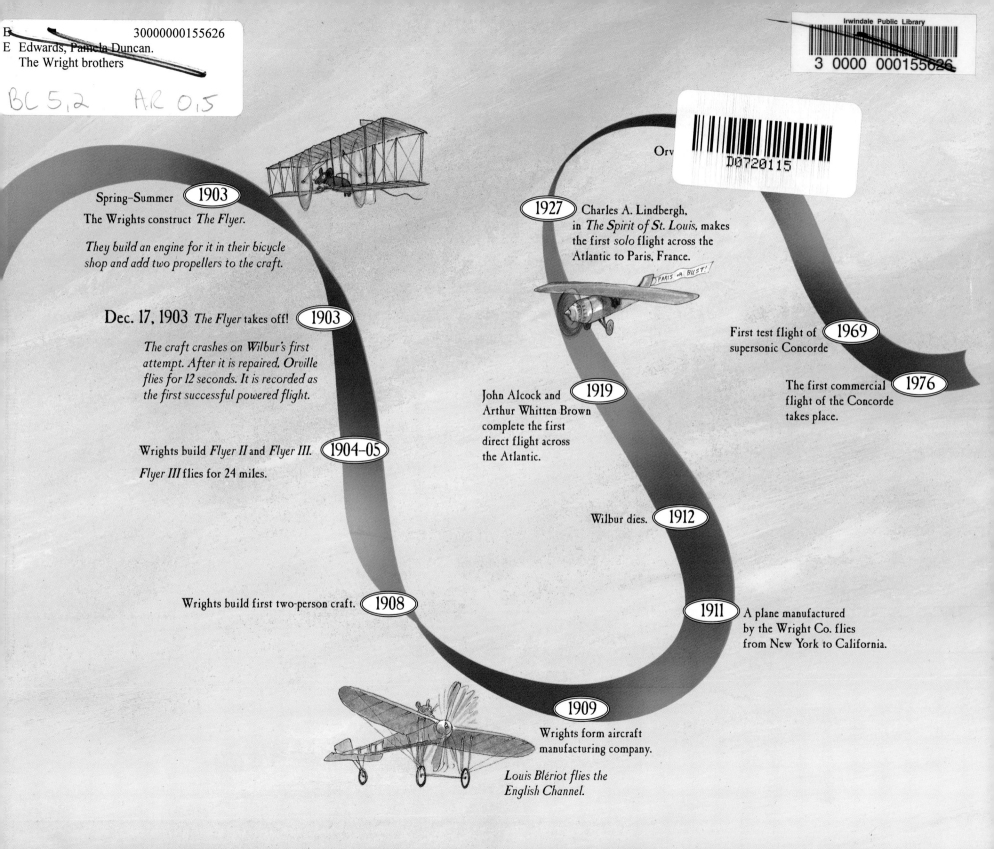

Spring–Summer 〔1903〕

The Wrights construct *The Flyer.*

They build an engine for it in their bicycle shop and add two propellers to the craft.

Dec. 17, 1903 *The Flyer* takes off! 〔1903〕

The craft crashes on Wilbur's first attempt. After it is repaired, Orville flies for 12 seconds. It is recorded as the first successful powered flight.

Wrights build *Flyer II* and *Flyer III.* 〔1904–05〕

Flyer III flies for 24 miles.

Wrights build first two-person craft. 〔1908〕

〔1909〕 Wrights form aircraft manufacturing company.

Louis Blériot flies the English Channel.

Orv

〔1927〕 Charles A. Lindbergh, in *The Spirit of St. Louis,* makes the first *solo* flight across the Atlantic to Paris, France.

PARIS or BUST!

John Alcock and Arthur Whitten Brown complete the first direct flight across the Atlantic. 〔1919〕

Wilbur dies. 〔1912〕

〔1911〕 A plane manufactured by the Wright Co. flies from New York to California.

First test flight of supersonic Concorde 〔1969〕

〔1976〕 The first commercial flight of the Concorde takes place.

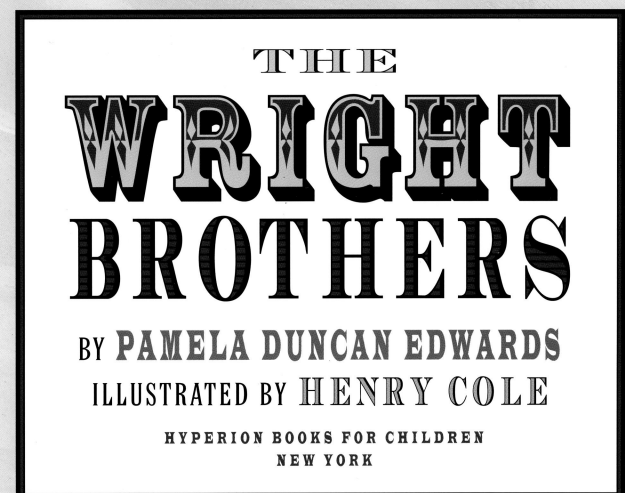

THE WRIGHT BROTHERS

BY PAMELA DUNCAN EDWARDS

ILLUSTRATED BY HENRY COLE

HYPERION BOOKS FOR CHILDREN
NEW YORK

First Edition

1 3 5 7 9 10 8 6 4 2

Printed in Singapore

This book is set in 18-point Caslon Antique.

The illustrations on the jacket, pages 24–25, 30–31, and 34–35 are all adapted from photographs taken by the
Wright brothers, used courtesy of the Wright State University Special Collections and Archives.

Library of Congress Cataloging-in-Publication Data on file.

ISBN 0-7868-1951-0 [trade ed.]

ISBN 0-7868-2682-7 [lib. ed.]

Visit www.hyperionchildrensbooks.com

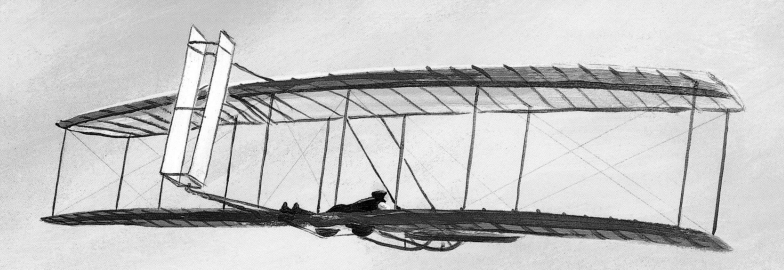

To Jo and Brian Falconer,
who have flown more miles around the
world than anyone I know
—P.D.E.

To Demmy, a great brother
and a great friend
—H.C.

This is the sky, high and wide,
which was conquered in flight in 1903.

Maybe someday mice will fly!

This is a toy that whirled through
the sky, high and wide,
which was conquered in flight in 1903.

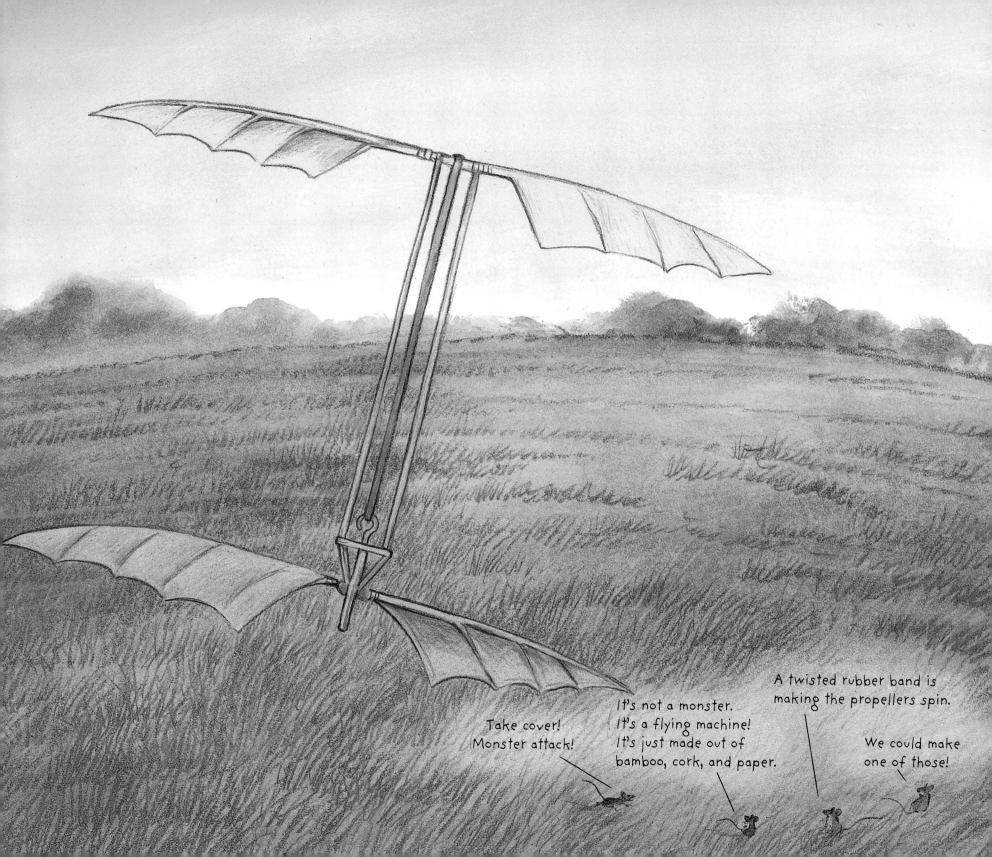

These are the Wright boys, Wilbur and Orville,
whose interest in flying was sparked by a toy that
whirled through the sky, which was conquered in flight in 1903.

I think the bigger the model,
the more power it needs.

It's okay when we make it small,
but if it's bigger, it doesn't fly properly.

Wilbur and Orville
keep trying to copy
the toy. We've made one, too!

Boy! This flying stuff is
harder than it looks!

This is a printing press designed by the brothers,
whose interest in flying was sparked by
a toy that whirled through the sky,
which was conquered in flight in 1903.

These boys are great inventors!
They've made a lathe to turn wood!
And a machine to fold
the newspaper!

We've made a press, too!
Get your *Mouse News* here!

I want to be
Food Editor!

When they grew up,
they published a
newspaper, *West Side
News*. Then they opened
a printing shop.
Now they've opened a
bicycle shop.

I'm practicing for
The Tour de Ohio!

This is the bicycle shop opened by Wilbur and Orville years after making a printing press designed by the brothers, whose interest in flying was sparked by a toy that whirled through the sky, which was conquered in flight in 1903.

Even though they're into designing bikes, they're still dreaming of making a flying machine.

These are the buzzards, soaring and dipping over the bicycle shop opened by Wilbur and Orville years after making a printing press designed by the brothers, whose interest in flying was sparked by a toy that whirled through the sky, which was conquered in flight in 1903.

These are the wings curved for lift, a secret of flight
revealed by the buzzards soaring over the bicycle shop
opened by Wilbur and Orville, years after making
a printing press designed by the brothers,
whose interest in flying was sparked by a toy
that whirled through the sky, which was conquered
in flight in 1903.

See how the curved wing
forces air underneath.

There's more air under
the wing than on top,
so it lifts the wing up.

Hey! I've got it!
When birds twist
their wingtips,
it balances them.

That bird's looking
straight at me!

Now we're ready to build a
mouse-carrying machine!

This is the kite, climbing and bobbing, inspired by the wings
of the buzzards soaring over the bicycle shop opened by Wilbur and Orville
years after making a printing press designed by the brothers,
whose interest in flying was sparked by a toy that whirled through the sky,
which was conquered in flight in 1903.

See! When they twist or "warp"
the wingtips, it helps the
machine ride the
wind currents.

I'm getting packed.
Will I need more
than one suitcase?

This is one of the gliders based on the kite, inspired by the wings of the buzzards soaring over the bicycle shop opened by Wilbur and Orville years after making a printing press designed by the brothers, whose interest in flying was sparked by a toy that whirled through the sky, which was conquered in flight in 1903.

I can't believe how big Orville and Wilbur's glider is.

We've put an elevator in front just like the Wrights did, to help the pilot steer up and down.

Well, ours is big, too. It's got to carry a mouse!

I've packed two pairs of underpants. I'm not sure how long this journey's going to take.

This is the beach in North Carolina where they tested the gliders
based on the kite, inspired by the wings of the buzzards soaring over
the bicycle shop opened by Wilbur and Orville years after making
a printing press designed by the brothers, whose interest in flying
was sparked by a toy that whirled through the sky,
which was conquered in flight in 1903.

Kitty Hawk's a good place to test
because the winds are usually just right.

Good thing there aren't many
trees to bump into, and there's
nice soft sand to land in.

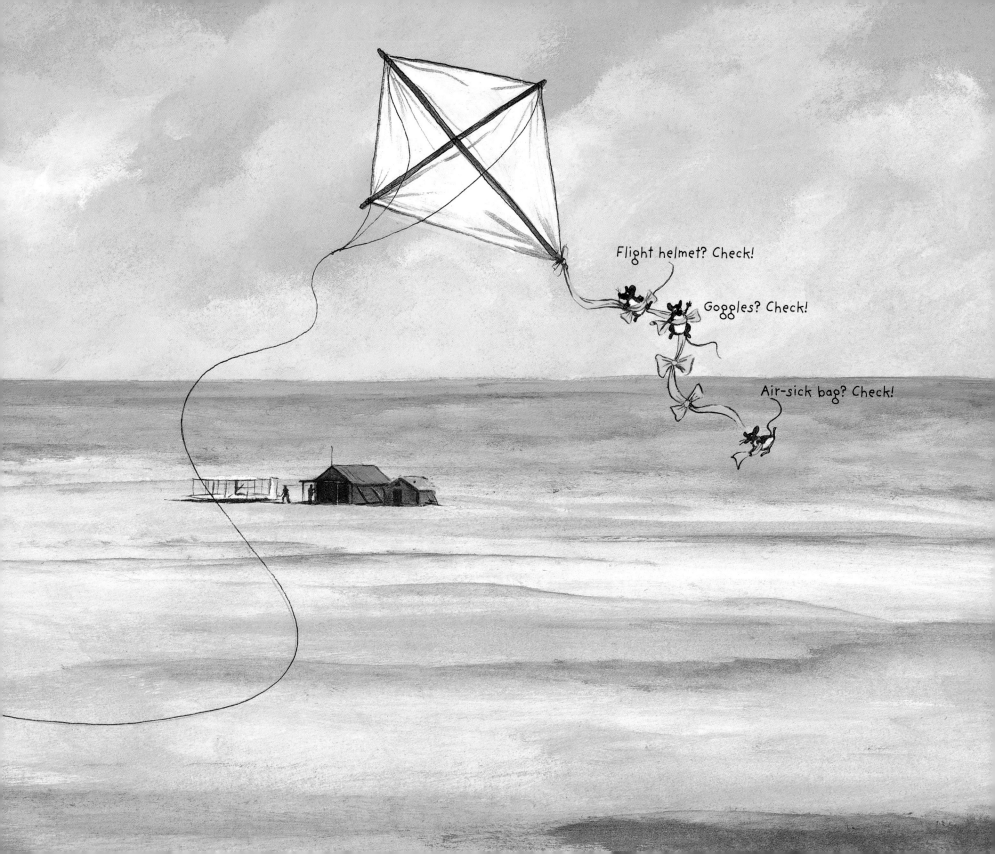

These are the many attempts to take off from the beach where they tested the gliders
based on the kite, inspired by the wings of the buzzards soaring over the bicycle shop
opened by Wilbur and Orville years after making a printing press designed by the brothers,
whose interest in flying was sparked by a toy that whirled through the sky,
which was conquered in flight in 1903.

Uh-oh! It's okay
when we fly
straight, but we
can't turn.

We're going to have to keep
experimenting with different
wing shapes.

I'm sick of waiting.
I might take a
train instead.

Wilbur and Orville
never give up.
Neither should we.

This is the craft that eventually flew after many attempts
to take off from the beach where they tested the gliders
based on the kite, inspired by the wings of the buzzards
soaring over the bicycle shop opened by Wilbur and Orville
years after making a printing press designed by the brothers,
whose interest in flying was sparked by a toy
that whirled through the sky, which was
conquered in flight in 1903.

Orville and Wilbur built a wind
tunnel behind the bike shop.
They drove air
through it onto
miniature wings
until they found
which shape was best.

The movable tail rudder
means we'll be able to make turns.

It needs an engine! Have
you guys got an engine?

Mayday!
Rock ahead!

This is the engine built by the Wrights following their success
with the craft that eventually flew after many attempts
to take off from the beach where they tested the gliders
based on the kite, inspired by the wings of the buzzards soaring
over the bicycle shop opened by Wilbur and Orville
years after making a printing press designed by
the brothers, whose interest in flying was sparked
by a toy that whirled through the sky,
which was conquered in flight in 1903.

Orville and Wilbur couldn't
find a light-enough engine,
so they've made their own
in their bike shop.

Will my suitcase fit
in the overhead bins?

This is THE FLYER making its maiden voyage,
powered by the engine built by the Wrights following their success
with the craft that eventually flew after many attempts to take off
from the beach where they tested the gliders based on the kite,
inspired by the wings of the buzzards soaring over the bicycle shop
opened by Wilbur and Orville years after making a printing press
designed by the brothers, whose interest
in flying was sparked by a toy
that whirled through the sky,
which was conquered in flight in 1903.

Orville managed to fly the
first-ever airplane. Yeah!

It was a clever idea
to use two light propellers
instead of one heavy one.

Excuse me, what
time will you be
serving lunch?

And these are the triumphs of THE AGE OF FLIGHT,
which was born with THE FLYER, powered by the engine
built by the Wrights following their success with the craft
that eventually flew after many attempts
to take off from the beach where they tested
the gliders based on the kite inspired by the
wings of the buzzards soaring over
the bicycle shop opened by Wilbur and Orville
years after making a printing press designed by
the brothers, whose interest in flying was sparked
by a toy that whirled through the sky,
which was conquered in flight in 1903.

Boeing B-17
"Flying Fortress"

Spirit of St. Louis
(Ryan "Special")

Boeing B-29

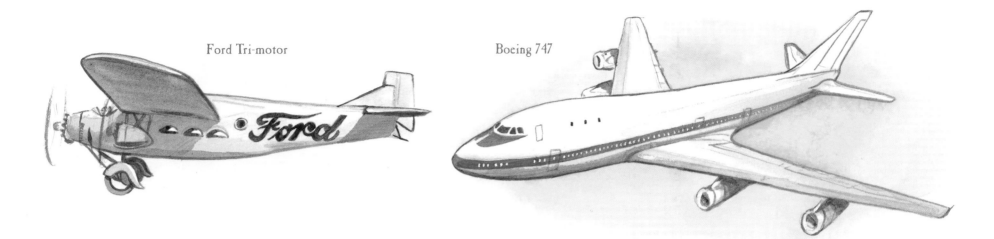

Ford Tri-motor

Boeing 747

Douglas DC-3

Mustang P-51

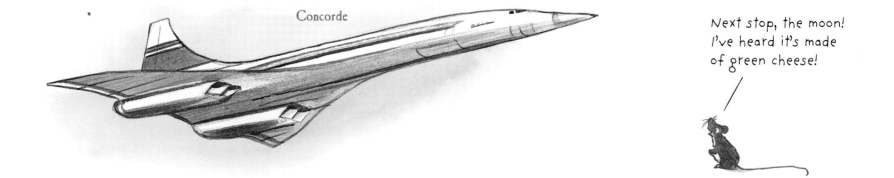

Concorde

Next stop, the moon!
I've heard it's made
of green cheese!

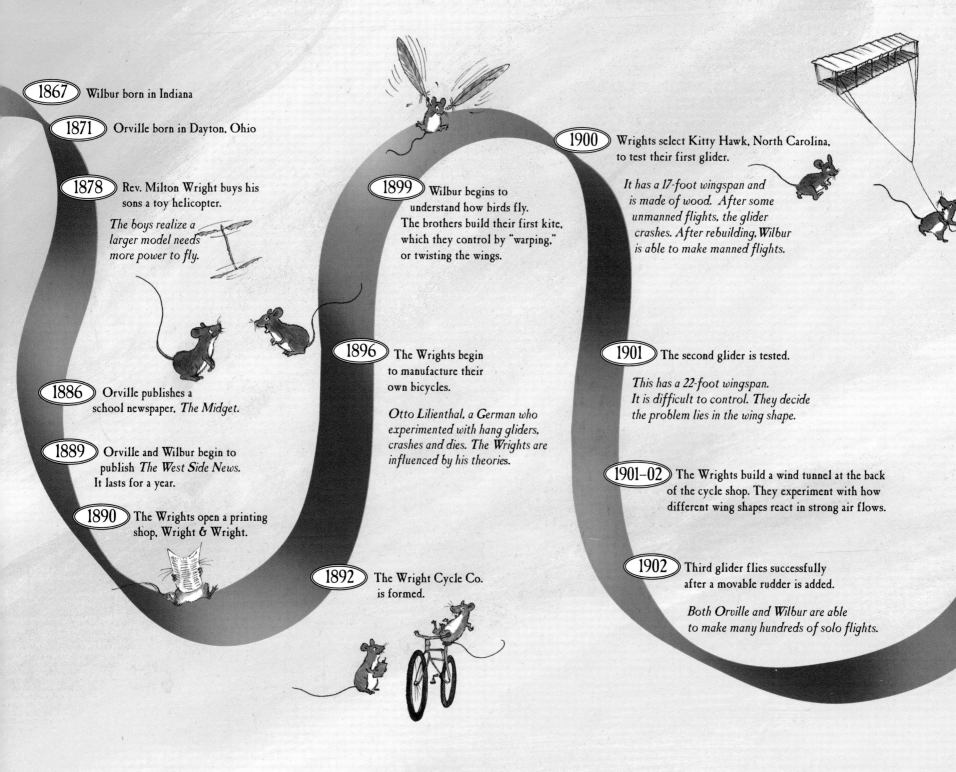

1867 Wilbur born in Indiana

1871 Orville born in Dayton, Ohio

1878 Rev. Milton Wright buys his
sons a toy helicopter.

*The boys realize a
larger model needs
more power to fly.*

1886 Orville publishes a
school newspaper, *The Midget.*

1889 Orville and Wilbur begin to
publish *The West Side News.*
It lasts for a year.

1890 The Wrights open a printing
shop, Wright & Wright.

1892 The Wright Cycle Co.
is formed.

1899 Wilbur begins to
understand how birds fly.
The brothers build their first kite,
which they control by "warping,"
or twisting the wings.

1896 The Wrights begin
to manufacture their
own bicycles.

*Otto Lilienthal, a German who
experimented with hang gliders,
crashes and dies. The Wrights are
influenced by his theories.*

1900 Wrights select Kitty Hawk, North Carolina,
to test their first glider.

*It has a 17-foot wingspan and
is made of wood. After some
unmanned flights, the glider
crashes. After rebuilding, Wilbur
is able to make manned flights.*

1901 The second glider is tested.

*This has a 22-foot wingspan.
It is difficult to control. They decide
the problem lies in the wing shape.*

1901–02 The Wrights build a wind tunnel at the back
of the cycle shop. They experiment with how
different wing shapes react in strong air flows.

1902 Third glider flies successfully
after a movable rudder is added.

*Both Orville and Wilbur are able
to make many hundreds of solo flights.*